Little Rabbit Goes to School

HARRY HORSE

PUFFIN

For Elliot

PUFFIN BOOKS
Published by the Penguin Group: London, New York, Ireland, Australia, Canada, India, New Zealand and South Africa
Penguin Books Ltd, Registered Offices: 80 Strand, London WC2R 0RL, England

www.penguin.com

First published 2004
Published in this edition 2006
5 7 9 10 8 6 4
Text and illustrations copyright © Harry Horse, 2004
All rights reserved
The moral right of the author/ illustrator has been asserted
Manufactured in China

ISBN 978–0–140–56894–3

This edition published in 2008 for Index Books Ltd

When Little Rabbit woke up he knew that it was
a special day. Today was his first day at school.

Little Rabbit got Charlie Horse up out of bed. "Come on, Charlie Horse," said Little Rabbit. "You have to go to school."

He brushed Charlie Horse's tail and tied on a red ribbon.

He took Charlie Horse along to show Mama.

"Now we are big," said Little Rabbit proudly, "we are going to school."

"Maybe Charlie Horse should stay at home with me," said Mama.

"I don't think wooden horses go to school."

But Little Rabbit would not listen.
"No, Mama," he said. "Charlie Horse
wants to go to school."

Mama gave Little Rabbit his lunch box and
told him not to open it till lunchtime.
"I won't, Mama," cried Little Rabbit.

Little Rabbit skipped
along after his brothers and sisters.
"Come along, Charlie Horse," said
Little Rabbit. "Don't be late for school."

Soon Charlie Horse needed
to stop for a little rest.

He wanted to open the
lunch box and take a look inside.

But he didn't like the lettuce
sandwiches so Little Rabbit
had to eat them. And he
didn't like the carrot cakes so
Little Rabbit had to eat them too.

"Come along, Little Rabbit!"
called his brothers and sisters.
"We'll be late for school."
  "It's Charlie Horse, he's making me late!"
said Little Rabbit. "Come along, Charlie
Horse, stop making me late."

School was much bigger than Little Rabbit thought. His new teacher Miss Morag was very pleased to see him. She *did* like Charlie Horse.

Miss Morag showed Little Rabbit his new classroom.
He was very shy. Everybody turned to look at him
and Charlie Horse.

"This is Little Rabbit," said Miss Morag.

Miss Morag sat down and read them
a story called *The Bad Rabbits* and even
though it was a good story, Little Rabbit
could not keep Charlie Horse still.
Charlie Horse wanted to gallop
over the fields.

He galloped across Benjamin . . .

he galloped over Rachel . . .

he even galloped over Miss Morag's shoes. Little Rabbit pulled him back.

Miss Morag let Charlie Horse rest on her desk
while Little Rabbit painted a picture.

After painting, they sang a song. It was called,
"If You Need a Friend Just Whistle".
Little Rabbit liked singing. Miss Morag said
he was a good whistler too.

But she didn't like it when Charlie Horse
jumped off the table and danced,
and she made Charlie Horse
sit in the corner for the
rest of the song.

Next they made little cakes. But Charlie Horse
was naughty and jumped in the cake mix.

Miss Morag did not like Charlie Horse in the cake mix.
She had to give him a bath.

Then the little rabbits began to play games.
They scampered and hopped in the
meadow, they dug holes and they
chased each other through
the long grass.

But Little Rabbit played alone with Charlie Horse.
He did not share him with Benjamin.
He did not let Rachel play with him either.
"Charlie Horse does not want to play
with you," said Little Rabbit.

Miss Morag rang the bell for lunch. All the rabbits
opened their lunch boxes. But when Little Rabbit
looked for his, he began to cry.

"What's the matter, Little Rabbit?"
asked Miss Morag.

"Somebody has eaten my lunch," cried
Little Rabbit, "and now I have none."

"You can have some of mine," said Benjamin.

"Don't cry, Little Rabbit, you can have
some of mine too," said Rachel.

Little Rabbit shared lunch
with his new friends.

When they'd finished he let them play with Charlie Horse.

"Charlie Horse likes you best," said Little Rabbit.

After lunch Miss Morag took some of the little rabbits on
a nature walk. Charlie Horse came along too.

"Couldn't we just leave Charlie Horse behind?" said Miss Morag.

"No, Miss," said Little Rabbit. "Charlie Horse likes
nature walks too."

On the way, Charlie Horse found a beautiful flower.

Miss Morag would like that flower, thought Little Rabbit.

So he let go of Benjamin's hand and followed Charlie Horse instead.

"Look what we found, Miss Morag!" said Little Rabbit.

But when he looked round, nobody was there.

"Where is everybody?" cried Little Rabbit.

Even with Charlie Horse he felt all alone.

Little Rabbit dragged Charlie Horse along a path in the woods.

He lost a shoe.

His coat got caught
on a prickle bush.

"This is all your fault, Charlie Horse,"
said Little Rabbit. "You made me lose my way.
Now I shall never find my way back."

Then Little Rabbit remembered the song that
Miss Morag had taught him and began to sing it.
"If you need a friend just whistle," sang Little Rabbit.
His song rang out in the dark woods.

Just as he began to whistle that's when
he heard Miss Morag calling him.

Little Rabbit ran.

Miss Morag picked Little Rabbit up
and they all went back to school.

When they got back to school, Mama and Papa were waiting for him, ready to go home.

And on the way, Little Rabbit told them all about school
and, best of all, his new friends.

"I can't wait to go to school again," said Little Rabbit, "but tomorrow Charlie Horse can stay at home with you, Mama. He's too naughty for school."

"What a good idea," said Mama.